D0411070

Lancashire Library Services	
12163937	
PETERS	JF
£11.99	20-Jul-2011

ARGUS

Michelle Knudsen

illustrated by

Andréa Wesson

WALKER BOOKS
AND SUBSIDIARIES
LONDON · BOSTON · SYDNEY · AUCKLAND

Squid life cycle

Sally's class was doing a science project. Mrs Henshaw handed out the eggs.

"Mine looks different," said Sally.

"Now, Sally," said Mrs Henshaw, "don't be difficult. Some eggs just look different."

The children kept their eggs warm in their brand-new desk-top incubators. Soon the hatching began.

"I see a beak!" one boy shouted.

"I see one, too!" the girl next to him called out.

Sally's egg wobbled. A tiny crack appeared. Then another. Something poked out a little bit of shell.

"Is that a beak?" one boy asked.

"I don't think so," said Sally.

The cracks in Sally's egg widened. Slowly, something emerged.

It was **green**.

And *scaly*.

And it had *big yellow eyes*.

"Mine looks different," said Sally.

The others gathered round to look. "Yuk," they said.

"Now, children," said Mrs Henshaw, "don't be difficult. Some chicks just, er, look different — that's all."

Sally named her chick Argus.

The class weighed and measured all the chicks. They took new measurements every day. Then they made line graphs showing the results.

All the other children's graphs showed short diagonal lines. Sally's graph ... didn't.

Growth Chart for Fluffy

for Butter

Next the children drew pictures of their chicks to put up on the walls. All the other children's pictures were cute and yellow and very much alike. Sally's picture … wasn't.

"Good work, children," said Mrs Henshaw. "Now let's investigate what our little chicks like to eat."

"Mine likes seeds!" said one boy.

"Mine likes beetles!" said another.

"Mine is trying to eat the other chicks," said Sally.
Mrs Henshaw rushed over and rescued them.

As the days passed, the chicks grew bigger. Argus was the biggest of them all. He stopped trying to eat the other chicks. He started trying to eat the children instead.

"Mrs Henshaw!" the children complained.

Mrs Henshaw rushed over and rescued the children.

The class began taking their chicks outside to peck in the grass at break. Argus wasn't very good at pecking. He chewed a giant hole in the ground with his teeth.

The other chicks all fell into it.

"Mrs Henshaw!" the children complained.

Mrs Henshaw rushed over and rescued the chicks. Sally and Argus had to move to a different part of the grass.

Later that afternoon, Sally went up to Mrs Henshaw.

"I don't think my chick is ... really working," she said quietly.

"Now, Sally," said Mrs Henshaw, "don't be difficult. Just go and mark your chick's height on the wall with the others."

The other children knelt down to mark their chicks' heights. Sally had to use the stepladder.

The next day at break, Sally led Argus to his special area. Mrs Henshaw had marked it off with orange cones for safety. Sally sat against the fence and watched the other chicks. They were all the same: cute and small and feathery and fluffy. The children chased them about, picking them up and stroking their soft little heads. Sally couldn't even reach Argus's head unless he was lying down.

The bell rang for the end of break. Sally sighed. She turned round to get Argus.

He wasn't there.

Sally looked round the playground. She ran to the gate and looked up and down the street. There was no sign of Argus anywhere.

"Oh, no!" cried Sally. She started to run back to class. Then she stopped.

Why was she so upset? With Argus gone, Mrs Henshaw would probably let Sally share one of the other children's chicks. She could make graphs that looked just like everyone else's. She wouldn't have to sit by herself at break. She could stop being different all the time.

Sally lined up to go inside with the others. She waited to feel relieved. She waited to feel happy.

She kept waiting while she followed the other children down the hallway and back into the classroom.

She waited while she went back to her seat. But she still didn't feel happy or relieved. She felt sad. And worried. What if Argus was scared and lost? He was out there somewhere, all alone.

Slowly, she raised her hand.

"Yes, Sally?" asked Mrs Henshaw.

"It's Argus," Sally said. "He's gone!"

Then she burst into tears.

The other children gathered round. They held their chicks tightly. "Don't cry, Sally," they said. "We'll help you look for him."

"Yes," said Mrs Henshaw firmly. "If there's one thing your chick is good at, it's standing out. We'll find him!"

She took down some of Sally's drawings and handed them out to the class.

They searched the area near the school. They showed the drawings to everyone they met. But no one had seen Argus. Sally got more and more worried. What if they never found him?

Suddenly, they heard a scream. *"Aaaaah!"* someone said. "What is that?"

There was Argus, trying to peck for insects
in someone's front garden.

"Argus!" Sally cried. She ran over and threw her arms round him.

"Our lawn!" said the people whose lawn it was.

"Thank you for finding our lost little chick," Mrs Henshaw said.

"But what about these holes?" asked the lawn owners.

Mrs Henshaw handed them an orange cone. "Don't be difficult," she said. Then she quickly led the children back to school.

My Chick:

eats dirt
sleeps
gets in trouble

How much I love Argus!

Sally

Sally's chart that afternoon was the best one she'd ever made. Mrs Henshaw gave it a big gold star. Sally looked at it hanging up with the other charts. "Mine looks different," she said. And she smiled.

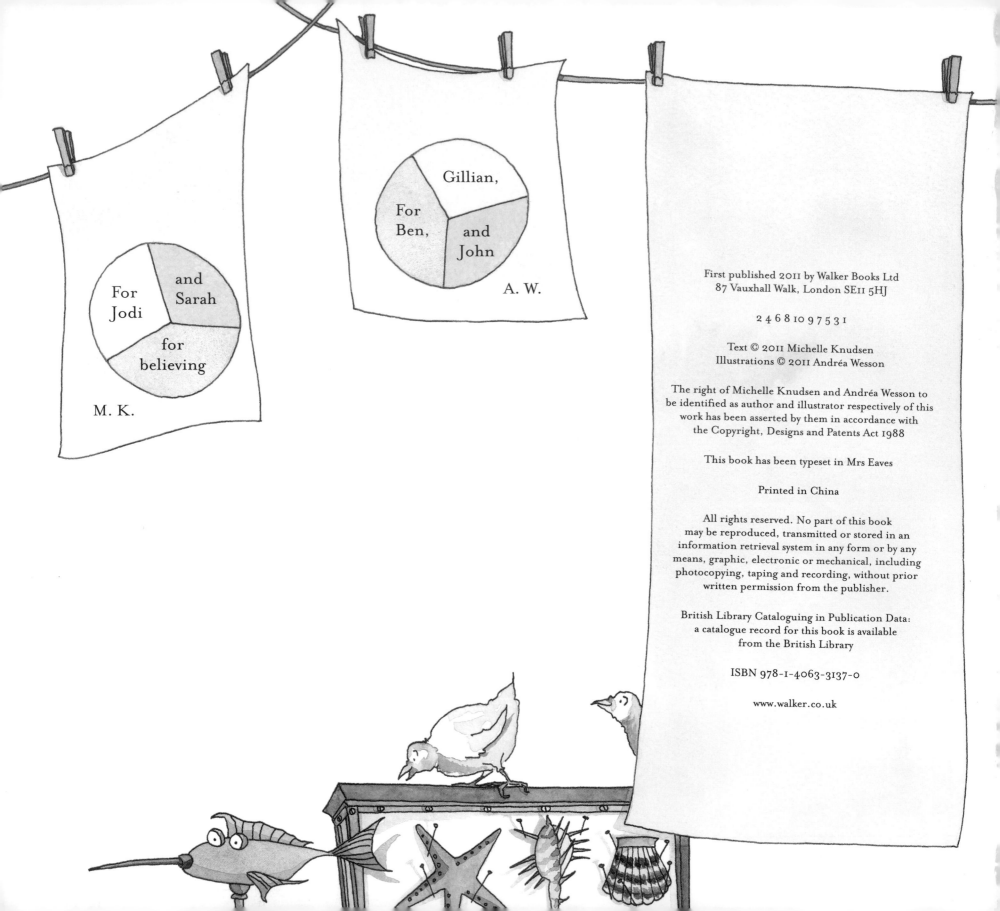

For Jodi and Sarah for believing

M. K.

For Ben, Gillian, and John

A. W.

First published 2011 by Walker Books Ltd
87 Vauxhall Walk, London SE11 5HJ

2 4 6 8 10 9 7 5 3 1

Text © 2011 Michelle Knudsen
Illustrations © 2011 Andréa Wesson

The right of Michelle Knudsen and Andréa Wesson to
be identified as author and illustrator respectively of this
work has been asserted by them in accordance with
the Copyright, Designs and Patents Act 1988

This book has been typeset in Mrs Eaves

Printed in China

All rights reserved. No part of this book
may be reproduced, transmitted or stored in an
information retrieval system in any form or by any
means, graphic, electronic or mechanical, including
photocopying, taping and recording, without prior
written permission from the publisher.

British Library Cataloguing in Publication Data:
a catalogue record for this book is available
from the British Library

ISBN 978-1-4063-3137-0

www.walker.co.uk